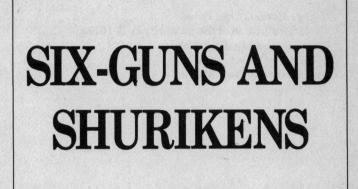

SIX-GUNS AND SHURIKENS

Other Teenage Mutant Ninja Turtle books available in Yearling Books:

TEENAGE MUTANT NINJA TURTLES

SIX-GUNS AND SHURIKENS

D A V E   M O R R I S

Illustrated by Phil Jacobs

A YEARLING BOOK

Published by
Dell Publishing
a division of
Bantam Doubleday Dell Publishing Group, Inc.
666 Fifth Avenue
New York, New York 10103

This work was first published in Great Britain by Yearling Books,
Transworld Publishers Ltd.

ISBN: 0-440-40392-8

Printed in the United States of America

June 1990

10 9 8 7 6 5 4

OPM

HEROES IN A HALF SHELL

Fourteen years ago a group of four ordinary turtles that had dropped into the storm drains beneath New York were found by Splinter, a master of the skill of ninjutsu, the ancient Japanese art of stealth and espionage.

Then . . . a leakage of radioactive goo exposed Splinter and his pets to mutating chemicals. Splinter turned into a giant talking rat, while the turtles became the Teenage Mutant Ninja Turtles—his wacky, wisecracking, crime-fighting ninja pupils.

With their human friend, April O'Neil, ace reporter on the Channel 6 TV News, the Turtles fight for what's right and foil the nefarious schemes of the Shredder, Splinter's evil renegade student.

Meet Leonardo, the coolly efficient sword-swinging team leader. Meet Donatello, the expert when it comes to machines; his swishing quarterstaff lays out his foes like bowling pins. Meet Raphael, the prankster, whose wry humor sees the team through perilous situations while his twin daggers send enemies fleeing in panic. And meet Michaelangelo, who's a master of the flying kick and the karate punch and is prepared to use them on anyone who gets between him and a pizza!

All kinds of weird things get washed up in the Turtles' den, in the sewers below New York. There was the time a gift-wrapped lady's hat from Saks Fifth Avenue turned up lodged against a grating beside Michaelangelo's bunk. He gave it to April as a birthday present, but of course she wasn't too impressed. After all, who wants a hat that's been in sewer water for a week?

Anyway that was another story. But it goes to show why none of our heroes was very surprised when Michaelangelo came in one evening clutching an old copper lamp covered in mud.

"Hey, dude, where'd you get the flowerpot?" said Raphael.

"Can't you guess, Raph?" put in Donatello. "Another bit of jetsam, Mike? You must think we're opening a junk shop here."

Michaelangelo put the lamp down proudly and glared at them. "It isn't a flowerpot and it isn't a jetsam—whatever that is! It's a lamp, and since it's made of copper, it's probably worth quite a bit. It might be an antique."

Raphael came over to sniff the dirty lamp, then pinched his nose. "Phew! I don't know about it fetching a high price, dudes, but it sure has a high old smell."

Michaelangelo snatched up the lamp protectively and growled, "You wait and see. Once I've polished it up, it'll look fine on the kitchen table."

"And if there's ever a power failure, we can even make some use of it," said Leonardo.

"Yeah," said Mike before he realized Leo was ribbing him.

"Oh, go on, Mike," continued Leo. "We're just kidding, aren't we, guys? Clean it up a bit and then it'll make a radical desk lamp for Master Splinter."

Michaelangelo brightened up at the thought. Master Splinter was out of town for a few days, but they had all heard him complain that the weak light bulb over his desk made his eyes hurt. It would be an excellent present to give him when he got back. All that evening while the others were watching TV, Mike sat on the arm of the sofa and polished the lamp. Before too long it was gleaming like new, and even the sarcastic Raphael had to admit that it looked like more than just an average piece of junk. "I wonder who threw it away?" he mused.

"I guess the owner just dropped it into a storm drain by accident," said Leonardo. "That's how *we* ended up down here in the first place, right, guys?" They all nodded. None of them could remember those early days before a mutating chemical gave them human intelligence, but Splinter had told them the story.

Raphael was looking through the TV listings. "There's a *Kung Fu* rerun at eight o'clock. We may as well watch the cowboy film till then, okay?" Since no one had any objections, he switched channels. The film had already started, and the action was in full swing. They watched as a stagecoach careened down a hill out of control, the driver slumped dead in his seat from a gunshot wound. One of the passengers was trying to climb around to take the reins, while two others kept up a gun battle with the Indians pursuing them.

The Turtles were immediately cheering in excitement. "Come on, get those reins!" "Who *are* those guys?" "The Indian chief's riding in with a tomahawk!" "Watch out!"

"Boy, those were the days," said Michaelangelo, still absentmindedly polishing his lamp. "Gunfighters, cowpunchers, and wild tavern brawls. I wish we could have seen the Wild West for ourselves."

Poof! No sooner had Mike said the words than the whole room vanished around them. There was a flash of light, and the Turtles suddenly found themselves in a dry cactus-grown gulch like a scene from any classic Western. Since the sofa on which they had been sitting vanished along with the rest of the room, they all went sprawling.

"Ooof!" said Leonardo. "Who swiped the sofa?"

"Never mind that," said Raphael, picking himself up and dusting the sand off his shell. "Who swiped our whole den?"

Michaelangelo went over to pick up the lamp, which he had dropped in surprise. "We must be dreaming. This is just like my wish that we were back in the Wild West. Oh no, look—the lamp's dented, dudes!"

The other three looked at him, then at one another. Donatello was the first to work it out. "A lamp polished . . . a wish granted . . ." He snapped his fingers. "Of course, guys! Mike, give that lamp another rub, will you?"

"Aww, gee, look at this dent . . ." was all Michaelangelo could say.

"Mike," Leonardo told him, "rub it!"

As Michaelangelo wiped the dust off the lamp, another strange thing happened. A plume of green smoke curled out of it and swirled around to form a thick column in front of them. As the four watched in amazement, the smoke began to spin around and around like a whirlwind. As it spun faster, they could see a figure taking shape in the middle of the cloud. In less than a minute the column of smoke had vanished and in its place was a muscular, golden-skinned man wearing green breeches and a green turban. He stopped spinning and immediately fell over out of giddiness.

"A genie!" exclaimed the Turtles in unison.

"Talking turtles!" exclaimed the genie. He got to his feet and stood with arms folded across his massive chest. For a moment he gave our ninja the fiercest look they had ever seen, and Leonardo was on the point of ordering them to attack. Then the genie's gaze alighted on the lamp Michaelangelo was holding, and he immediately bowed deeply. "Master," he said. "It's you who have polished the lamp in which I was imprisoned so many centuries ago. Your wish is my command."

"Like the wish that brought us back here to the Wild West?" put in Leonardo before Mike could reply.

"Exactly," boomed the genie. "By the terms of my imprisonment, which were set upon me in ancient times by King Solomon, I can grant the owner of the lamp three wishes. Your first wish has already been granted. I have transported you back in time to the year 1890, to a place west of the Pecos. Nowhere has ever been wilder or wester than this."

Michaelangelo had taken a few seconds to realize what the genie was telling them. Now he could hardly speak for excitement. "S-so what kinda wishes can we have?"

The genie bowed again. "Anything, masters. Whatever you desire."

"Anything? *Absolutely* anything?"

"Absolutely anything."

"Wow!" gasped Michaelangelo. "In that case, I wish for—"

"Mike!" yelled Leonardo. "Stop him, dudes!"

The others leaped toward Michaelangelo, but they were too slow. In the instant before Donatello could clamp a hand over his mouth, Michaelangelo managed to blurt out, "I wish for the biggest pizza I ever saw!"

The genie waved his arms, and a pizza the size of a manhole cover appeared at Michaelangelo's feet. It had every conceivable topping, from anchovies and avocado slices to mango and mozzarella. He bent down and stared at it, drooling, oblivious of his friends' anger.

"You dope, Mike!" growled Leonardo. "You just wasted our second wish."

Michaelangelo glanced up in the act of raising a slice of pizza. It was at least three times wider than his mouth. He tried to cram it in while considering what Leonardo had said. "Uh . . . yeah, Leo, but why worry?" He looked at the others. "What's the matter, dudes? We still have another wish, don't we?"

Raphael stormed up and grabbed the pizza slice from him. "What do you use for brains, your stomach? We need the last wish to get back home."

Michaelangelo slapped his head and groaned. "Oh no! You're right, dudes. I really goofed up this time."

"So what's new?" grunted Raphael. He tore the pizza slice in half and handed one bit back to Michaelangelo.

Leonardo came over and took the lamp. "Well," he said, "there's no sense in crying over spilled milk. Mike, pick up the pizza carton. It cost us our free wish, so we might as well take it back with us.

The rest of you, gather around. Genie, this is our third and final wish: I want—"

"Hey, wait, Leo," said Donatello. "Why go rushing back to the present day? Since we've ended up in the Wild West, there surely isn't any harm in taking a look around before we head home."

Leonardo seemed dubious. "I don't know . . ."

Michaelangelo and Raphael were on Donatello's side. "Come on, Leo, where's your sense of adventure? Aren't you at least curious to see what the old cowboy days were really like? If we rush off back home now, we'll miss the chance of a lifetime."

"Yeah," said Michaelangelo. "Who knows? We might even meet Wyatt Earp or Billy the Kid."

"Or John Wayne," added Raphael drily.

Leonardo threw up his arms. "All right, all right, I give in. We'll spend just one day here in the Wild West and then we're going back. And I'm hanging on to this lamp for the time being. Genie, can you slip back inside?"

"Sure," said the genie, turning into a wisp of smoke and curling back into the lamp. "Just give it a rub when you want your last wish," said a tinny voice from inside.

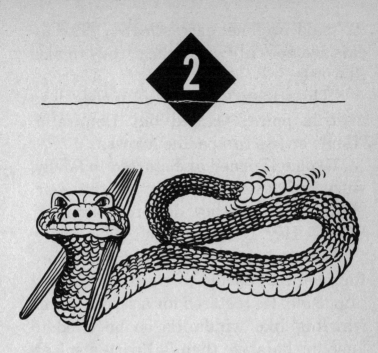

It was almost toward dusk. The Turtles made their way north along a dirt road until they reached a shallow stream. Beside the ford a weather-beaten old sign was still just readable despite its peeling paint: *Black Rock, 1 mile,* it declared. Underneath this, someone had carved with a penknife, *Tern back if yerv got any sense.*

"That looks very welcoming, doesn't

it?" said Raphael sarcastically. "The locals are not only unfriendly, they're also illiterate."

"The stream's only a few inches deep at this point," called out Donatello. "Come on, we can paddle across."

Raphael turned and started to follow, with the others bringing up the rear. "What do we care how deep it is, anyhow? We're— Hey, Don, watch out!"

Donatello hadn't time to move before Raphael had darted forward and shoved him aside. He teetered for a second, arms whirling like windmills as he tried to keep his balance, then fell with a splash in the deeper water off the pebble road. Even as he did so, Raphael drew one of his sai-daggers and plunged it down into the ground at the exact spot where Donatello's foot had been an instant earlier.

Donatello rose, spluttering, and waded back to the shore. "Can't you ever quit clowning around?" he snapped at Raphael.

"Who's clowning?" At that moment

there was a sound like someone shaking a bag of stones. They all followed Raphael's gaze and saw the reason why he'd pushed his friend aside. A mean-eyed rattlesnake glared up at them, hissing and shaking its tail angrily. Fortunately it was securely caught between the prongs of Raphael's sai.

Donatello stared at it in horror. "I take it all back, Raph. You probably saved my life."

Raphael grunted. "Aww, don't be a drip." Since Donatello was still dripping from his fall in the river, the joke helped everyone to calm down after their shock.

"Get rid of it, then, Raph," chuckled Leonardo. "I've a hunch that compared with some of the townsfolk of Black Rock, that rattler may turn out to seem as mild as a mouse."

Raphael flung the rattler off downstream with a deft flick of his wrist, then sheathed the sai and followed the others. As they approached the town, acting on a silent signal from Leonardo, they left the path and slipped into the bushes.

"We'll wait till after sunset," whispered Leonardo. "No telling how the locals might react to the sight of us."

They all nodded. Leonardo, as Master Splinter's best pupil, was their unofficial leader. He never missed an opportunity to hone the team's stealthy ninja skills.

Michaelangelo never missed an opportunity to eat. "Anyone want this slice with the dill pickle on it?" he whispered, hauling out the huge pizza box.

The sound of footsteps came from further down the path, heavy boots crunching the gravel. "Shhh," warned Leonardo at once. He listened intently, then held up two fingers to indicate that two people were approaching.

Less than a minute had gone by when the two men came in sight. As bad luck would have it, they stopped right next to the bush where Leonardo and the others lay in hiding. The Turtles studied them in the twilight: one a big thick-necked, stomping fellow with a belly like a beer barrel, the other a lithe ferret of a man in a fancy coat. Both wore pistols on their belts.

"Hold up, will ya, Slim," said the big man. "You been shootin' along like a greased gopher with his hind end on fire."

The smaller man stopped and came back, spreading his hands. "Sorry, Tex, you know how it is—I'm more of a city dude. I'll face any man in a showdown, but the open country makes me nervous. I keep thinking there's some scorpion or rattler under the next stone I kick over, and—"

A coughing came from the bushes, abruptly choked off. Michaelangelo grinned sheepishly at his friends. "Sorry, dudes," he breathed. "I swallowed an olive pit . . ."

"Shhh," hissed Leonardo, ducking back after taking a glance. "I think they heard you."

Slim was pointing at the bushes. "Did you hear that, Tex? Did you hear it? There's someone there, I tell you." He drew his revolver, and there was an ominous click as he cocked it. With a steely glint in his eye, he crept toward the bush where the Turtles crouched in concealment.

Tex sat down on a boulder, pulled off his boot, and started to massage his toes. "Goldarnit, must get myself a pair that fit better. Will you just calm yourself, now, Slim? You're jumpier than a long-tailed cat in a room full of rockin' chairs."

Slim had got right up to the bush where the Turtles were hiding and was just reaching out to push the branches aside with the barrel of his gun. The Turtles tightened their grip on their weapons, ready to spring into action, but just then Michaelangelo had an idea. He made a rattling sound deep in his throat, a perfect imitation of the rattlesnake they'd encountered half an hour before. Ventriloquism was another of the ninja skills that Splinter had taught them.

Slim almost jumped out of his fancy clothes. He went scurrying off back to

where Tex was sitting, shaking like a leaf. "It's a ruh—ruh—rattler, Tex! What did I tuh—tuh—tell you?"

Tex put on his boot and got slowly to his feet. "And what did I tell *you*, pardner? You got to get a grip, boy. You stay this jumpy, and you ain't gonna be no use to me when the time comes. It's a good thing Bad Bob ain't here yet. If he saw you actin' up like this, he'd fill you fuller of lead than a church roof."

"He isn't going to see me like this, Tex. I'm clearing out first thing in the morning—heading back to Barbary. You don't need me to handle old Clampett, after all. The two of you can do the job easy."

Tex smiled in a lazy, rather sinister way and took hold of Slim's frilled shirtfront, then hauled him up until they were eye-to-eye. "I'm gonna pretend I didn't hear that. I'd hate to think of you runnin' out on a job now, Slim. Bad Bob would hate it even more, I reckon, and then Grandpa Clampett wouldn't be the only one to wind up in a pine box. You get my drift?"

Slim swallowed a gulp. "Sure, sure, Tex. I was just kidding. The rattler made me nervous, that's all, but you know you can count on me."

Tex put him down and smoothed his crumpled vest. This apparently friendly gesture seemed even more threatening than his previous aggression. "I know that, Slim," he said quietly. "Bob's turnin' up in a couple days. Now we've scouted out ol' man Clampett's place, there ain't no need for you ta leave town again till we go to do the job. Haul yourself over to the saloon with me and we'll stack up a couple of bottles of sippin' whiskey, okay?"

They set off down the path toward town. The Turtles watched until they were out of sight, then emerged from the bushes.

"I get the feeling those were the guys in the black hats," said Raphael.

"What do you mean?" asked Michaelangelo, still munching on his pizza slice. "They weren't wearing hats."

"The bad guys, dude—and I mean bad as in *bad*. So what are we waiting for? Let's follow them."

Leonardo put a hand on his arm. "No, forget them for now. You heard them say they were just going to the saloon for the evening. It seems like the third member of their gang, this Bad Bob character, must be the boss. They're waiting for him to arrive in town before they get up to whatever mischief they have planned."

Michaelangelo and Raphael had stopped listening at the word *saloon*. They were imagining a wild party like those they'd seen in any number of Westerns. Fortunately, Donatello agreed with Leonardo: "We'd better backtrack and see if we can find out where those two guys have just been," he said. "It sounded to me like they're planning to murder someone!"

Night had fallen by the time the Turtles had found their way to the Clampett ranch. It lay off the main trail about two miles from the town of Black Rock. There was an old log cabin, big but rather run-down, with a rickety windmill outside for bringing water up from a well. In a corral out the back they saw several scrawny horses. Hens wandered to and fro, pecking at the dry ground.

"Keep to the shadows," urged Leonardo. "We're here to help old Mr. Clampett, but if he's feeling trigger-happy, we might never get the chance to explain that."

As if on cue, the door of the cabin creaked open, and a shaft of lantern light shone out. They could just make out a tall, gangling figure carrying a shotgun. Beside him was a mangy old dog that gave a halfhearted growl and then slunk out onto the porch to lie down.

"Who's out there?" called the old man. "Tex, if that's you and yer fancy city 'slinger, you'd better take a hike. I already gave you my answer. If you keep on hanging around like an unwelcome sniff o' skunk, yer liable to find the whiskey leakin' out of yer gut the next time you take a drink. You got that?

Leonardo walked forward into the lamplight with his hands up. He kept his keen gaze focused on the old man's trigger finger. At the slightest sign that he was about to shoot, Leo was ready to leap to one side.

The dog took one astonished look at Leonardo, whined, and ran back into the cabin with its tail between its legs. The old man screwed up his eyes and peered through glasses as thick as beer bottles. After a moment he relaxed and lowered his gun. "A youngster, eh? Well, I don't see none too good these days, but I can see you ain't that varmint Tex. You better come in, youngster."

"There's four of us," replied Leonardo. He beckoned the others forward: "Come on, guys."

Bud Clampett blinked at them near-sightedly as they stepped into his cabin. The dog was cowering behind a wooden bench. "Short fellers, ain't ya?" said Bud, peering at them like a scrawny old owl. "Mite green around the gills, too. You should eat up all your victuals, young-sters."

"Turtles don't have gills," said Dona-tello.

Bud was clattering around pouring coffee into tin mugs, so he did not hear this. As he came back and handed each of them a mug, Michaelangelo said, "And we've got plenty to eat, too. A genie gave us a huge pizza. Do you want a slice?"

Bud scratched his head. "Jeannie? Jeannie Grant at the general store? She gave you a huge piece of what?"

"No, no," said Michaelangelo. "This was a magic genie, and he gave us a huge piece of pizza. P-I-Z-Z-A. Here, try a slice."

Bud took the pizza and munched at it dubiously. "Bread and cheese is all this is, youngster. Landsakes, it's no wonder you need feedin' up if that's all your folks give you. Well, you just sit right there and ol' Bud will fry you up some bacon and beans."

As he started to cook supper, the Turtles began to question Bud about the two thugs who had paid him a visit earlier. "Them two curs?" he spat. His dog growled at this remark, and he added, "Sorry, old girl, no offense. What I mean is, those two are the lowest, orneriest critters west of the Pecos. An' that includes anything you might find under a stone too. Their names are Tex Mac-Andrew and Slim Jim Daniels, an' they work for a low-down mean son-of-a . . ." He glanced at the dog. ". . . they work for a low-down mean son-of-a-pig called Bad Bob."

Michaelangelo had been munching on pizza the whole time Bud was cooking, but it didn't seem to have affected his appetite. The moment a plate of bacon and beans was put in front of him, he began to devour it as though he hadn't seen food in a week. "So what did they want with you?" he asked Bud between mouthfuls.

Bud peered at him. "Landsakes, if you young whippersnappers go gulpin' your grub down like that, you'll get indigestion fer sure. Don't your folks feed you no real food?"

"We don't have any folks," said Donatello. "We're orphans."

"Master Splinter looks after us,"

added Leonardo, "but he eats only rice and sushi—that's raw fish."

Bud banged the table. "Raw fish! What kind o' diet is that for growin' boys?"

"Master Splinter's a rat," put in Raphael.

"I'll say he is!" shouted Bud. "Well, listen, you boys can stay here with me as long as you like. Ain't no need for you to go back to this raw fish and piece o' cheese, or whatever ya call it. Me and Molly'd be glad of the company, to tell the truth." As he said this, the old dog wandered out from behind the bench and curled up at his feet. She still kept one eye open and fixed on the Turtles, though.

"Uh, listen, Mr. Clampett . . ." Leonardo tried to think of the right words, but it was difficult to avoid using phrases like *time travel* and *magic lamp*, which Bud obviously wouldn't understand. In the end he said, "That's a kind offer, but we have to get back home to New York in a day or so. Still, as long as we're hanging around, we might be able to help you with Bad Bob and his men."

Bud shook his head sadly. "I don't think so, son. These fellas are just about as desperate a bunch o' villains as you're likely to meet anywhere. I used to be a sheriff, you know, in my younger days. We're going back quite a few years, of course, when I could see farther than a few inches ahead o' my nose. I was a pretty-darn-fair shootist too. It was me that plugged Snake-eye McSlattery and his band of outlaws—six bullets, six men laid out dead outside the jail. An' back in the War, those Yankees used to run like jackrabbits when they saw Bud Clampett gunnin' for them. No-good varmints like that Tex wouldn't have dared come around threatening me back in them days. No sirree!" Bud's weak old eyes misted over as he allowed his thoughts to drift back to the days of his youth.

Leonardo pulled him back out of his reverie. "So just what are they threatening you about, Mr. Clampett?"

"I'll tell you, son. I been settled here nigh on twenty years now. I do a bit o' farming, but mainly I pan for gold up in the hills. Get a bit now and again, too, but nothing you'd call a fortune; just enough to buy a few extras now and then. Anyhow, this is the age o' the railroad. The rail company's driving a track clear through to the West Coast, an' one day they looked at their plans, then at the map, and some pencil pusher noticed that ol' Bud Clampett has his homestead plum across the middle o' where they want to lay their track. They came around and made me an offer to buy the place, but I'm too old to move—and anyways their offer didn't include nothing for the odd bag o' gold dust I might pan in. So I got out my rifle and I told 'em what they should do with their offer. I waited about a month, then Tex and Slim came around earlier this evening and they made a new offer."

The Turtles nodded. "We can guess the kind of thing," said Leonardo. "So the rail company paid Bad Bob and his pals to chase you off."

"Why don't you just go to the sheriff and tell him the whole story?" asked Donatello.

"It's clear you ain't never met the sheriff of Black Rock, son. He's as partial to bribes as other men are to strong liquor. The rail company will have paid him to be off duty when Bad Bob comes callin', you can be sure of that."

The Turtles looked glumly at one another, all thinking the same thing. It was plain to see that Bud had no intention of leaving his homestead. It was equally obvious that his pride would make him face up to Bad Bob and his bullies, even though he could no longer see well enough to shoot through a barn door at ten paces. He was in trouble.

The Turtles were all keen to get back home by now, having seen as much as they wanted to of the Wild West, but they could not just walk away and leave Bud in danger. Their ninja oath meant that they should always protect the weak against the strong. Leonardo chose his words carefully: "Say, Mr. Clampett, we don't have to head back to New York for a few days yet. Maybe we could stay here after all. We'd help with chores and things."

"I could get that old wind pump running more smoothly," put in Donatello. "Maybe even wire up some kind of dynamo so you could have electric light."

"Old-fashioned oil light's good enough fer me, son, but thanks fer offerin'. No offense, but I ain't got a whole deal of time fer some of the fandangled ideas you folks bring from back east. It's all a mite too modern fer me."

"He's right," whispered Raphael to the others when Bud went to fetch more coffee. "A hundred years too modern!"

The next day, on the pretense of helping with various chores, the Turtles were able to spy out the lay of the land around Bud's homestead. Fortunately there were enough boulders and bushes to give them plenty of opportunities for cover. If the gunslingers came to threaten Bud after dark—and that seemed quite likely, this close to town—then the conditions would be ideal for using ninjutsu.

"Remember that our skill is the art of invisibility," Leonardo told the others as they went about their work. "We stay hidden, because an enemy cannot fight a foe whose existence he doesn't even suspect."

"You sound just like Master Splinter, Leo," grumbled Michaelangelo as he shifted a heavy barrel up onto the porch. "Why don't you give me a hand with this instead of lecturing us all?"

Leonardo came over to see what Michaelangelo was doing. He was fixing one of the struts supporting the barrel so that it could be quickly tugged away using a concealed string. When this happened, the barrel would be sent rolling down off the porch. "As long as I time it right, those thugs will be bowled over like tenpins," he said to Leonardo.

Similar traps were being set by the others at strategic points around the cabin. Whichever way Bad Bob and his men came, the Turtles were ready for them. By midafternoon, while taking a break to finish the last slices of Michael-angelo's megapizza, they agreed on their plan. "Obviously we have to make it seem to Mr. Clampett that he's handling these bullies by himself," said Leonardo. "He's a proud old man, and it's important to him to keep his self-respect."

"He's also a nearsighted old duffer," said Raphael, "so it shouldn't be difficult to fool him. We just have to make sure that Bad Bob and his men don't start firing too soon."

Donatello spoke up: "That's some-thing we can't be sure of. One stray bul-let, or even a ricochet, could spell trag-edy. On the other hand I have an idea . . ."

They huddled closer to hear Donatel-lo's plan. Later, after rummaging around Bud's wardrobe for half an hour finding some old clothes to use as a disguise, they set out toward town. Wrapped in long coats with hat brims pulled down over their eyes, our heroes were an odd sight. Bud only squinted at them from his rock-ing chair on the porch. "Goin' into town, fellas?" he said, chewing on a lump of tobacco.

"Only for a few hours," said Leonardo. "Just for a look around."

"Black Rock ain't no place you'd need more'n two minutes to look over, son. Still, I guess you city folks like to get a glimpse of the real West. We'll chow down at eight thirty, if'n you can be back by then."

The Turtles waved good-bye and set off down the trail leading to town. "Remember," said Leonardo to the others, "if anyone starts looking too closely at us, distract them and then make tracks. It wouldn't do for any reports of mutant turtles to get into the history books!"

"Hey, maybe that's where the idea of 'little green men' got started," said Michaelangelo. "Anybody brought the flying saucer?"

"I'm not kidding, Mike," said Leonardo sternly. "We have to be very careful while we're in the past. If we do anything to change things from the way they happened in history, it might affect the present day."

Raphael scratched his head. "That's a complicated thing to get into, dude. For a start, what if we hadn't turned up? Things would've gone very differently for old Mr. Clampett, I'm sure."

"Yeah," said Leonardo, "but I don't think something like that would change the future. He might've just got lucky, or the rail company might have changed their minds about where to lay the tracks. What I mean is we have to be careful not to say anything that would start people thinking in a way that's wrong for 1890. Also we mustn't leave anything lying around when we go back—a shuriken spike sitting in a Wild West saloon, or one of Donatello's gadgets turning up around Mr. Clampett's corral, that kind of thing. Any sign of something out of place for this period could change the future. And if *that* happens, we might wind up going back to a future where we never existed!"

"*Mondo bizarro,*" said Raphael. "It doesn't bear thinking about, guys."

Fortunately they did not have to think about it any longer, for they were now nearing the outskirts of Black Rock. As Bud had suggested, it was an unremarkable western town consisting of a number of wooden frame buildings connected by boardwalks. Several townsfolk, bustling about their business on the dusty main street, nodded politely at the four strangers. Black Rock had all the standard features seen in movies: the sheriff's office with a jail, the church, the smithy and stables, the bank, and the saloon. They particularly noticed the saloon because, as they walked up to it, a man came flying out through the swing doors. A moment later Tex appeared in the doorway to glower at the man, who picked himself up and ran off. "Haw haw!" laughed Tex. "That's one Yankee who'll check the bar for Rebs before he goes makin' toasts like that again." He went back into the saloon whistling "Dixie."

"You know what I'm thinking, dudes?" said Michaelangelo. "I'm wondering how tough and mean Bad Bob must be if he's even tougher and meaner than that guy."

They pushed back the doors and stepped inside. Since it was still late afternoon, the saloon was almost empty. An old cardsharp sat at a table nearby, an untouched glass of whiskey at his elbow, practicing his tricks. Two bored bar girls were lounging against a piano in the corner, one of them idly picking out a few notes of a honky-tonk tune. If the girls were hoping for Tex and Slim to buy them a drink, they looked as though they would be disappointed: the two ruffians were propped against the bar with bottles of beer in hand, chortling over some undoubtedly vile and vicious joke. The bartender, a short, tubby man with big startled eyes that made him resemble a pig, glanced at the disguised Turtles and then went on polishing the glasses.

The foursome walked up to the bar.

"Sir," Raphael called to the bartender in exaggeratedly formal tones, "four glasses of your finest lemonade, if you please."

"Lemonade?" barked Tex before the bartender could answer. "Well, haw, haw, haw! Ain'tcha got the stomach fer a real drink, sonny?"

"I beg to differ with you, sir," said Raphael. "It is well known that alcoholic beverages rot the brain."

"Raphael!" Donatello hissed behind his hand. "Don't provoke him."

"Don't worry, dudes," whispered Raphael. "I won't blow the plan. I just think this bully needs taking down a peg or two."

"Rot the brain, huh?" Tex belched and put his beer bottle down. "Well, maybe you're right and maybe you're wrong, sonny. But from the evidence I see before me, I'd say it's a sure bet that this here lemmy-nade stunts yer growth!"

Raphael coughed in mock politeness. "And it appears clear that whatever you regularly drink causes the belly to swell up like a barrel of wine and gives you a face like the hind end of a donkey."

Dead silence descended. There was the snap of one last card being turned over by the gambler, one last astonished plink from the piano keyboard, a whimper of dread from the bartender, and then absolute silence.

Tex's face reddened. It went through red and turned purple. His bushy eyebrows knitted together like storm clouds, and his eyes were like balls of lightning. A growl built up, starting as a soft rumble like thunder in the hills but quickly welling up until Tex's whole huge frame shook. One could almost imagine steam coming out of his nostrils. When he finally released his anger in an almighty roar, it rattled the glasses behind the bar and sent the other inhabitants of the saloon diving for cover: "Well, CRACK MY CHEEKS!" It was as though someone had let off a cannon. "It's plain you're just plumb tuckered-out-tired of livin', boy. And I'm gonna dig that grave fer you with my own two bare hands . . ."

Tex came at Raphael like a rampaging bull. Though probably less than half his opponent's size, the Turtle didn't flinch. At the last moment, as Tex's arm swung toward his throat, he whipped his sai-dagger from inside his coat, reversed his grip on the handle, and jabbed it down so that Tex's wrist was caught between the blade and one prong. Tex froze, then gave a yelp of pain as Raphael began to turn the sai—he either had to move or allow his trapped wrist to be dislocated. Tex was angry but not stupid. With a flip Raphael flung him over the bar, where he landed with a crash.

"Nice work, Raph," said Leonardo, "using the enemy's own strength against him."

"The bigger they are . . ." said Raphael with a smile as he sheathed his sai. Behind the bar Tex gave a groan but seemed in no hurry to get up immediately. Falling with the force of a hundred tons had knocked the wind out of him.

"Okay, Chuckles, I'm impressed by

your cheek," said Slim. He held his silver-plated, ivory-handled revolver in his left hand while carefully setting down the beer bottle in his right. "Now perhaps you'd like to show me what your fancy moves can do against a .44 Smith and Wesson."

"Hey, you long, thin streak of bacon!" called Michaelangelo. "Chew on these." Slim turned just as he was passing the gun into his right hand. He hadn't noticed Michaelangelo sidle over to the gambler's table and snatch up the deck of cards, which he now flung like a fistful of shuriken spikes. By reflex Slim put his hand up in front of his face, and the gun went off. The bullet shot through the chain that supported a chandelier above his head, and it fell, knocking him to the floor. As he struggled to push the broken chandelier away, Leonardo grabbed the others. "Come on, guys," he said. "You've had your fun, but now it's time we were out of here."

The Turtles were trained to move fast

and silently. By the time Tex and Slim had got to their feet, the saloon doors were swinging to and fro with a gentle creak. There was no sign of our four heroes.

The next day, just after noon, Bad Bob rode into town.

Dressed from head to foot in black, with silver buttons on his shirt and silver guns at his hip, he sat square in the saddle of his white horse. Townsfolk stopped what they were doing and stared when they saw him, then edged nervously away when they caught the cold gaze of his flint-hard eyes. They say that several old ladies, out on a shopping and gossiping spree, fell in a dead faint out of sheer terror when they rounded a corner and came face-to-face with him. Cats went stiff as wire brushes and spat, terrified, while dogs just fled with their tails between their legs. No one can say any of this for sure, though, because within two minutes of Bad Bob's riding into town the street was completely deserted.

He dismounted and tied up his horse's reins outside the saloon. Then, silver spurs jangling, he stepped up onto the boardwalk and pushed open the doors. The regular inhabitants of the bar were already there, even this early in the day. Already nervous from what they had witnessed the previous evening, they dived for cover at once.

Tex and Slim grinned weakly at their boss. Tex's wrist had been sprained, and he now wore a sling; Slim's head was bandaged where the falling chandelier had given him a nasty bruise.

Bad Bob squinted at them and removed the thin cigar from his mouth with one black-gloved hand. "Had some trouble?" he said menacingly.

"Hell, no, buh-buh-boss," stuttered Tex. He raised his arm. "You mean this? Just a brawl we got into with a couple of dozen hayseeds last night—ain't that right, Slim?"

Bad Bob strode at a measured pace to the bar. He glared at the cowering bartender, then at the beautifully polished wooden surface of the bar. Taking out a match, he struck it across the polish and lit his cigar. "You ought to take more care of your bar," he said to the bartender, nodding once at the resulting burn mark. "Give me a shot of that redeye."

The bartender turned to see which bottle of liquor Bad Bob was looking at. The next second he jumped like a jackrabbit when a gunshot rang out right behind him, shattering the neck of a bottle.

Bad Bob blew across the smoking barrel and holstered his gun. "On second thought," he said, "just hand me the bottle. Seeing as it hasn't got a cork, it'll only spoil otherwise."

"Ha, ha, ha," came Slim's rather forced laughter. "You sure are a hoot, boss."

Bad Bob took a swig from the whiskey bottle and crunched a few pieces of broken glass as though he thought they were a delicacy. Slim saw this and blanched. "And you are a brainless turkey, Daniels," said Bob. He turned to Tex: "You can stop grinning, MacAndrew. They haven't even invented the words that would describe *your* level of stupidity. How is it I can leave you two alone for just a few days, and when I come into town, I find you've got yourselves battered in a brawl?"

"But there was dozens of 'em, boss," protested Tex. "Them hayseeds, they insulted General Robert E. Lee. I won't take that from no man."

"No? Well you can shove your General

Lee, MacAndrew. Lee's a big pain, you got that? God made brighter blowflies than that Confederate monkey." Bad Bob narrowed his eyes and gave a frosty smile. "What do you say to that?"

Tex gulped. "Sure, boss, whatever you say. Guess the general weren't none too bright at that."

Bad Bob took a step closer, swishing the whiskey in his mouth. "You dumb Texan cowpoke," he said, growling. "You're lucky it's not your gun hand that got sprained, because then I would've blown your empty head clean off your shoulders. Now, I'm going to check into a room and get myself washed up. Stay out of trouble, you hear me? I want you two ready to do the job you're paid for when we go to visit old Clampett tomorrow."

News of Bad Bob's arrival spread across town like wildfire. By sunset it had also reached the Turtles, courtesy of a young errand boy who brought supplies from the general store out for Bud once a week.

"Well, that's all they've been waitin' fer, fellas," said Bud over supper. "I guess those shootists'll be payin' me a visit any day now." His dog, Molly, whimpered, and he patted her sadly.

"First," whispered Leonardo to the others as Bud cleared away the plates, "I think we'll pay them a visit."

Much later that night, when they were sure that most of the townsfolk would be asleep, the Turtles crept back into Black Rock. This time they were clothed in their traditional ninja garb. Moving as silently as shadows, they reached the back of the saloon. Above them was a balcony with open doors, which led to the guest rooms above the bar. Leonardo gave a signal, and Donatello cast a grapple hook up to snag the balcony. Within seconds they had climbed up the rope. The corridor off the balcony gave on to several rooms, but it was easy to find Tex's and Slim's: Using their ill-gotten wealth they had booked the grandest quarters available. The

Turtles split into two pairs and noise-lessly tiptoed up to where the two gun-slingers were sleeping.

Donatello leaned over Tex's snoring form and sniffed his breath. "No need to worry too much about waking him up," he whispered to Raphael. "He'll sleep for hours. Obviously they put away a whis-key bottle or two during the evening."

"Trying to drown their hurt pride, I wouldn't wonder, after the chewing out they apparently got from Bad Bob," whispered Raphael with a mischievous grin. He had taken Tex's gunbelt from where it hung on the back of a chair and was now replacing the bullets with blanks that Donatello had made earlier in the afternoon.

They rejoined Leonardo and Michael-angelo in the corridor between the two rooms. They had succeeded in making an equal substitution with Slim's gun.

"Getting at Bad Bob's gun might be more difficult," said Leonardo. "He's un-likely to be such a sound sleeper as these two. We might need something to distract him."

"No, we don't," said Donatello. He had taken out several slender bamboo rods that he had tucked into his belt, and was now fitting them together end-to-end. They slotted into place to form something like a long fishing rod. He fit a line and hook to the end. "Time for some fishing, I think."

Pushing Bad Bob's door open, Donatello reached into the room and neatly hooked a gunbelt off the dressing table. After quickly replacing the bullets with blanks, he replaced it in the same way. The black-clad figure on the bed had not stirred.

On the way back out Michaelangelo had an idea—or thought he did. "Hey, guys," he said as they dropped back down to the street. "Why don't we just call the genie and get him to fix everything up? It'd be safer, surer, and a heck of a lot less effort."

Raphael jumped on his back and

wrestled him boisterously. "Because someone not a million miles from here wasted a wish on filling his big stomach, that's why! We have only one wish left to get us home, remember?"

"Hey, quit fooling around, you guys!" ordered Leonardo. "You could still mess up the mission if you wake anyone now."

The others quieted down and followed Leonardo, grumbling about his bossiness. As they slipped away down the trail to Bud's house, Donatello glanced back toward town. Nothing was stirring in the moonlight. "Mission accomplished," he said. "And we've set up all our tricks around Mr. Clampett's place. All we can do now is wait for those guys to show up—and hope that nothing goes wrong."

At that precise moment an owl hooted. It was a bad omen.

Bud Clampett sat out on the porch the
next day with a rifle across his lap and a
revolver in his belt. "They're bound to
show their ugly faces 'round here today,
young fellas," he said to the Turtles. "I
appreciate your helpin' out around the
place an' all, but just you take care to be
outta the way when the shootin' starts."

Leonardo took the others off around
the back to have a last run-through of

their plan. "Mr. Clampett can't see details very clearly, but he can still tell where people are standing and so on. That means that if we make any of the bad guys fall over, we have to time it to coincide with his shots."

"I've got a sling here," said Donatello. "I can put a stone right between the eyes of one of those guys. I ought to be able to do that just as Mr. Clampett fires."

Raphael chipped in. "And I'll stay behind the water pump and signal you, Don, when he's about to pull the trigger. I've just got one question, though, Leo. We're not going to kill them, are we? So what do we do?"

"That's easy," Leonardo told him. "Once they're all out cold, we'll tie them up and put them across the backs of their horses—then point the horses west and slap their rumps. By the time Bad Bob and his men get loose, they'll be so humiliated and saddle sore that I guarantee they won't be coming back in a hurry."

"Look!" said Raphael. "Dust! There are riders coming, and we're not ready!"

"Quick! Back to the shack," shouted Leo, already running off. "We've got to get into position!"

Running around to the side of the house they saw Bad Bob and his two henchmen dismounting. Bud had come to the top of the porch steps and was leveling his rifle at them. Leonardo gestured for Donatello to get up on the roof—a good vantage point for sniping with his sling. Raphael sneaked off to hide behind the water pump, and the others took up their positions too.

"You'd better just get back on your horses and go back the way ya came, boys," said Bud to the three gunmen. "I ain't lookin' fer trouble, but I know how to dish it out if I have to."

Bad Bob puffed blithely at a cigar, his hands resting lightly on the handles of his guns. "Wouldn't matter none if you were looking for trouble or not, old man," he said. "You'd never see it anyway."

"You can't threaten me, you hound dog," said Bud. "No offense, Molly," he added to his faithful dog.

"Who's threatening?" Bad Bob drew both his guns and cocked them in one smooth motion. As he grinned, his eyes narrowed in a cold squint.

"We haven't come here to *threaten* you, Clampett," said Slim. He, too, drew his gun.

Tex chuckled and hefted his own revolver. "Hell, no, we did that last week. Ya didn't take notice at the time, so now we've come back ta kill ya."

"You can try." Bud raised the rifle and peered through his thick glasses. All he could make out at this distance were three hazy shapes. He took aim as best he could at the one dressed all in black.

The Turtles held their breath. Would their trick work? Or had the villains noticed the blanks in their guns?

Bad Bob had plenty of time to shoot before Bud's arthritic old hands had squeezed the trigger. Blam! His opening shot gave Tex and Slim their signal to open fire. Shot after shot rang out, merging together like a roar of cannon fire.

Bud was momentarily hidden in a blaze of gunshot flares and smoke. The three men stopped firing only when their guns were out of bullets.

They wore smiles of pure malice—but only for an instant. As the smoke cleared, they were amazed to see Bud still standing on the porch, shakily aiming his rifle, none the worse for wear. "Impossible!" gasped Bad Bob.

"Seems you fellas ain't the hotshot surefire gunslingers you thought you were," said Bud, looking through his rifle sight. "I recommend you hightail it outta here before I get riled."

Bad Bob's only answer was a snort of contempt. He pulled new shells from his gunbelt and began reloading his revolver. He was unaware that those shells, like the ones he and the others had just fired, were Donatello's blanks.

Bud could not see much, but he could see that the three villains were not backing off as he'd warned them. His aged rifle hiccupped a loud report as he pulled the trigger.

The shot went wide by several feet, but it did not seem that way. For the precise moment that Bud fired, Raphael gave the signal, and Donatello unleashed a slingshot from his concealed vantage point at the edge of the roof. Tex groaned and fell, a thin rill of blood curling down his forehead. He was only stunned, but it looked for all the world to Bad Bob and Slim that he had been shot dead.

"Daniels," said Bad Bob, "go in and finish the old sidewinder. I'll keep you covered."

"A pleasure, boss." Slim dropped his empty gun and took out a stiletto knife. "Come here, old-timer," he said, advancing in a fighting crouch toward Bud. "We're going to finish this close up and personal, like."

The planking of the porch creaked under Slim's foot as he stepped up. He failed to notice the strut holding a heavy water barrel against the wall, or the string tied around it. Just as Bud aimed a clumsy kick at his assailant, Michaelangelo, hidden behind a woodpile at the corner of the shack, tugged the string, and the barrel fell free. This all happened so fast that it looked as though Bud had deliberately kicked the strut away. Slim had time only to turn and gawk in surprise before the barrel careened over him like a steamroller, bowling him back off the porch. It rolled off down the hill, leaving him black and blue and in no shape to knife anyone. Michaelangelo winked and gave a thumbs-up to the other three Turtles.

"This is going beyond a joke," said Bad Bob with a growl. Before Bud could fire the rifle again, he emptied the chambers of his gun in the old man's direction. As before, the bullets had no effect. This time, though, he guessed the reason: "Blanks!"

"It's a poor workman that blames his tools," said Bud. "Looks to me like you're just findin' an excuse for plain poor shootin'."

"Poor shooting!" snarled Bad Bob.

"You senile old fool. I could've put a bullet between your eyes all the way from town. No, somehow somebody switched the bullets in my gun . . ."

"I think he's got the message," whispered Leonardo to the other Turtles with a grin. He signaled Donatello to be ready to use his sling if Bud took a shot. Then he heard something that made his heart skip a beat.

". . . Fortunately," Bad Bob was saying, "I always make a point of carrying a spare." He reached down and drew a .32-caliber pistol from a flap in his boot. It was small, but no less deadly than a full-size gun. He started to advance toward Bud, a grin of evil creased across his face.

The Turtles froze in shock. They hadn't known about this extra gun, still loaded with live ammunition. From being a kind of game the whole thing had now turned deadly serious.

"Don," called Leonardo up to the roof. "Drop him, quick!"

Donatello hesitated a moment too

long. Before he could take another shot with his sling, Bad Bob had reached the porch and stepped up. Even leaning out over the edge of the roof, Donatello could not get a clear shot. Nor were any of the Turtles' other traps near enough to help.

Raphael started to break cover. "He's going to kill old Mr. Clampett!" he said. "Quick, guys, we have to stop him."

Leonardo caught his arm. "But, Raph, if we step in now, he'll know that everything else was just our tricks!"

Michaelangelo did not hesitate. He knew what had to be done—what Master Splinter would expect him to do—even though it meant getting stranded in the past forever. Whipping out the copper lamp, he called into it: "Quick, genie. You've got to give Mr. Clampett back his old sharpshooting skills just for one last gunfight!"

Poof! There was a sudden flash of light across the shack. If Bud and Bad Bob noticed it at all, they thought it was just summer lightning.

What Bud *did* notice was that he suddenly felt years younger. What's more, he suddenly had a clearer view of the sneering black-clothed bully threatening him with a pistol.

"Time's up, oldster," said Bad Bob.

Bud grinned. "I'd say yours is, son." Swinging the rifle barrel up far faster than Bad Bob would have believed possible, he released five shots in rapid succession. The first sent Bad Bob's pistol spinning out of his hand. The second blew his black Stetson up into the air like a startled cat. The third and fourth ricocheted off his silver spurs, spinning them with jangling, discordant notes. And the last bullet snapped Bad Bob's suspenders without even tearing his shirt. As he ran off, clutching at his falling trousers, Bob had a chance to reflect that he really never had seen shooting as good as that. The rail company could keep their money—he'd sooner visit the devil himself than face Bud Clampett in a showdown again!

Tex and Slim were both coming to. Seeing their boss in full flight, they wasted no time figuring out what had happened and raced off after him, wailing like lost sheep. Molly chased them to the edge of the yard, barking enthusiastically. The four Turtles hugged each other boisterously, and Michaelangelo leaped into the air, punching out a victory salute. Then they headed around to see Bud again.

"Well, what'a ya know," said Bud as they came strolling up. "Pardners, you missed all the fun. I wasn't sure I still had it in me, neither."

Leonardo shook his head. "We saw it, Mr. Clampett. I don't think you're going to have any more trouble with the railcompany bosses. It'll be easier for them just to detour the tracks around Black Rock! Anyway, thanks for your hospitality, but we have to be on our way now."

"So long, fellas. An' be sure an' drop by if you're ever out this way again."

They waved Bud good-bye and started

to walk off. "I don't know where we're going," griped Raphael to the others. "I'm not disputing that you did the right thing, Mike, but we're stuck in the Wild West for good now."

"Sure," moaned Michaelangelo. "And I don't even think pizza's been invented yet. I wish we'd never found this stupid lamp." He threw the lamp down in a sudden frustrated rage, and it broke open against a rock.

Green smoke fizzed up into the air. The genie took shape out of the middle of the cloud, gingerly fingering a lump on his head. "Ouch!" he boomed.

Leonardo looked worried. Drawing his sword, he motioned for the others to get behind him. "I think you've really broken it this time, Mike."

The genie looked at them and beamed. "Not at all," he said cheerfully. "I'm free at last, and I have you to thank for it! Normally people just get their three wishes and then leave the lamp lying around for someone else to find a hundred years later. No one ever thinks of freeing you. It's not a lot of fun being a genie in a lamp, I can tell you."

"If it's fun you're after," said Michael-angelo, "then New York is the place you want to be. Parties, discos . . ."

"Pizza parlors," put in Donatello.

"Why not?" said the genie. "Yes, I think that would be a nice change—so step closer—uh, dudes, and let's see what the twentieth century has to offer!"

In a whirlwind of colored light the genie whisked them back to the present day. They were back in their familiar den, apparently only minutes after they had left it. "We're still in time for the *Kung Fu* episode," said Donatello, switching the TV channel. No one protested at missing the Western. They had had enough of cowboys and gunfights to last a lifetime.

The genie stood beside them. He had now magically clothed himself in the height of 1990 fashion and looked to be a very elegant foreign gentleman. "So," he said, "do I cut a fine figure? Is this any good?"

"Better than good, dude, it's real *bad*!" said Raphael.

"Our modern expressions may take some getting used to," said Michaelangelo when he saw the genie's puzzled look. "Anyhow, thanks for bringing us home after all."

The genie protested. "It is I who must thank you, my former master. Let me give you this as a token of my gratitude." He took a pizza box out of nowhere and handed it to Michaelangelo. "This is a never-ending pizza," he explained. "No matter how many times you take a slice from the box, it will always contain at least one more. Now, farewell!" And in the blink of an eye he was gone.

◆

Michaelangelo took his magical pizza box off to his own corner of the den. "Wait till I show this to Master Splinter," he told the others excitedly. But the next day they noticed that the box was gone.

"Hey, dude," called Raphael. "Don't hog the pizza all to yourself, huh?"

Michaelangelo looked up and shrugged. "Oh, that? I gave it away."

"You did *what*?" exclaimed Donatello.

"I don't believe it," said Leonardo.

"Yeah, I gave it to April for someone she knows at the soup kitchen," Michaelangelo said grumpily. "It wasn't worth keeping. You know, these genies are so out of touch—would you believe an everlasting pizza *with no pepperoni!*"

SOUP RIDES AGAIN!

Yearling Dell

Whether he's riding into trouble on horse-back or rolling into trouble on an outrageous set of wheels, Soup and his best friend Rob have a knack for the kind of crazy mix-ups that are guaranteed to make you laugh out loud!

☐ SOUP 48186-4 $2.95

☐ SOUP AND ME 48187-2 $2.95

☐ SOUP FOR PRESIDENT 48188-0 $2.50

☐ SOUP IN THE SADDLE 40032-5 $2.75

☐ SOUP ON FIRE 40193-3 $2.95

☐ SOUP ON ICE 40115-1 $2.75

☐ SOUP ON WHEELS 48190-2 $2.95

☐ SOUP'S DRUM 40003-1 $2.95

☐ SOUP'S GOAT 40130-5 $2.75